MEG UP THE CREEK

for Abigail

MEG up the CREEK

by Helen Nicoll
and Jan Pieńkowski

PUFFIN BOOKS

Meg Mog and Owl
went in a canoe

up the creek

and into the wood

Owl and Mog went hunting

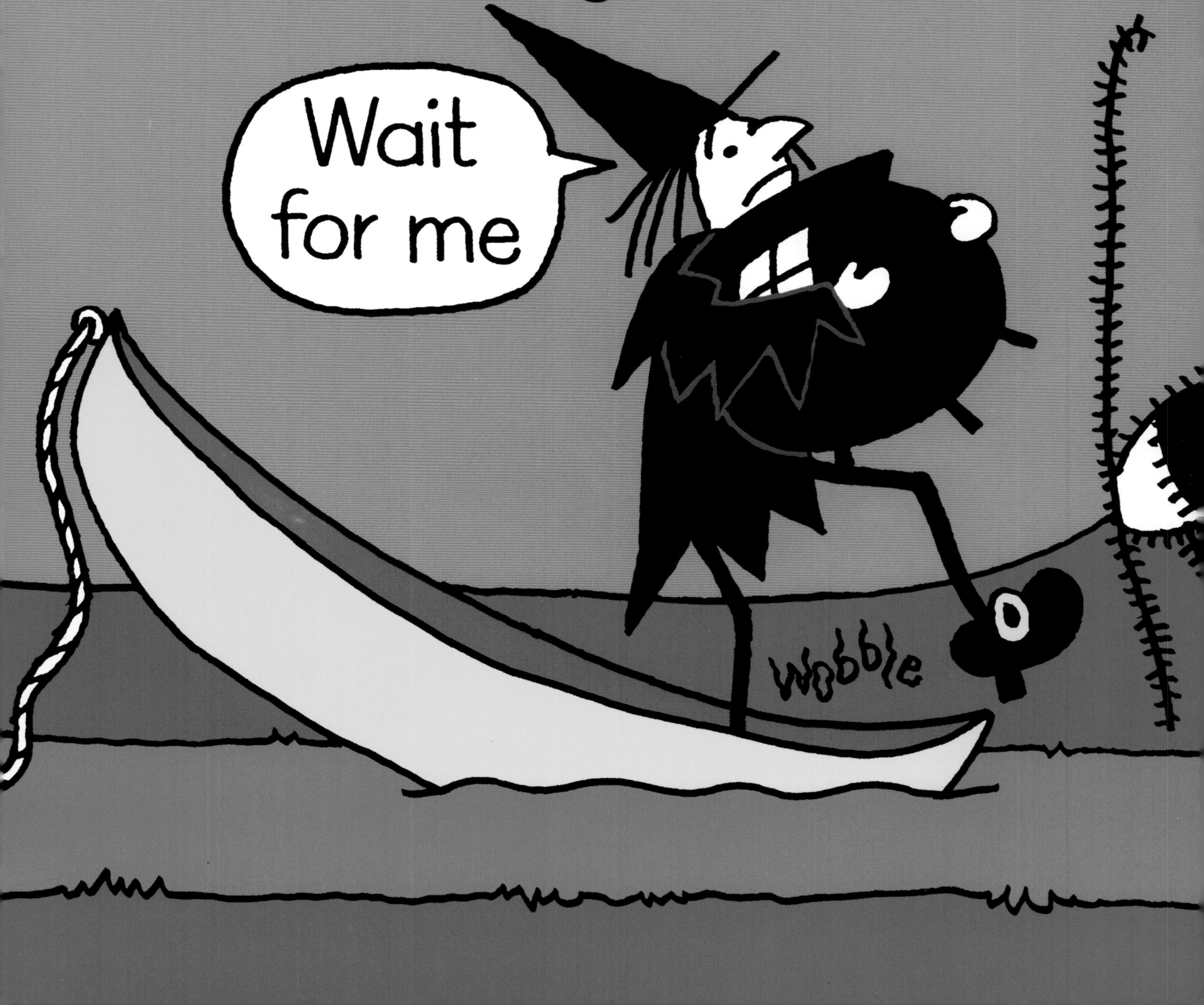
Wait for me
wobble

Tally ho!
Half for you half for me

POUNCE
Rats! Too late

That's mine!
And mine
Bon appétit

Owl went to find Meg

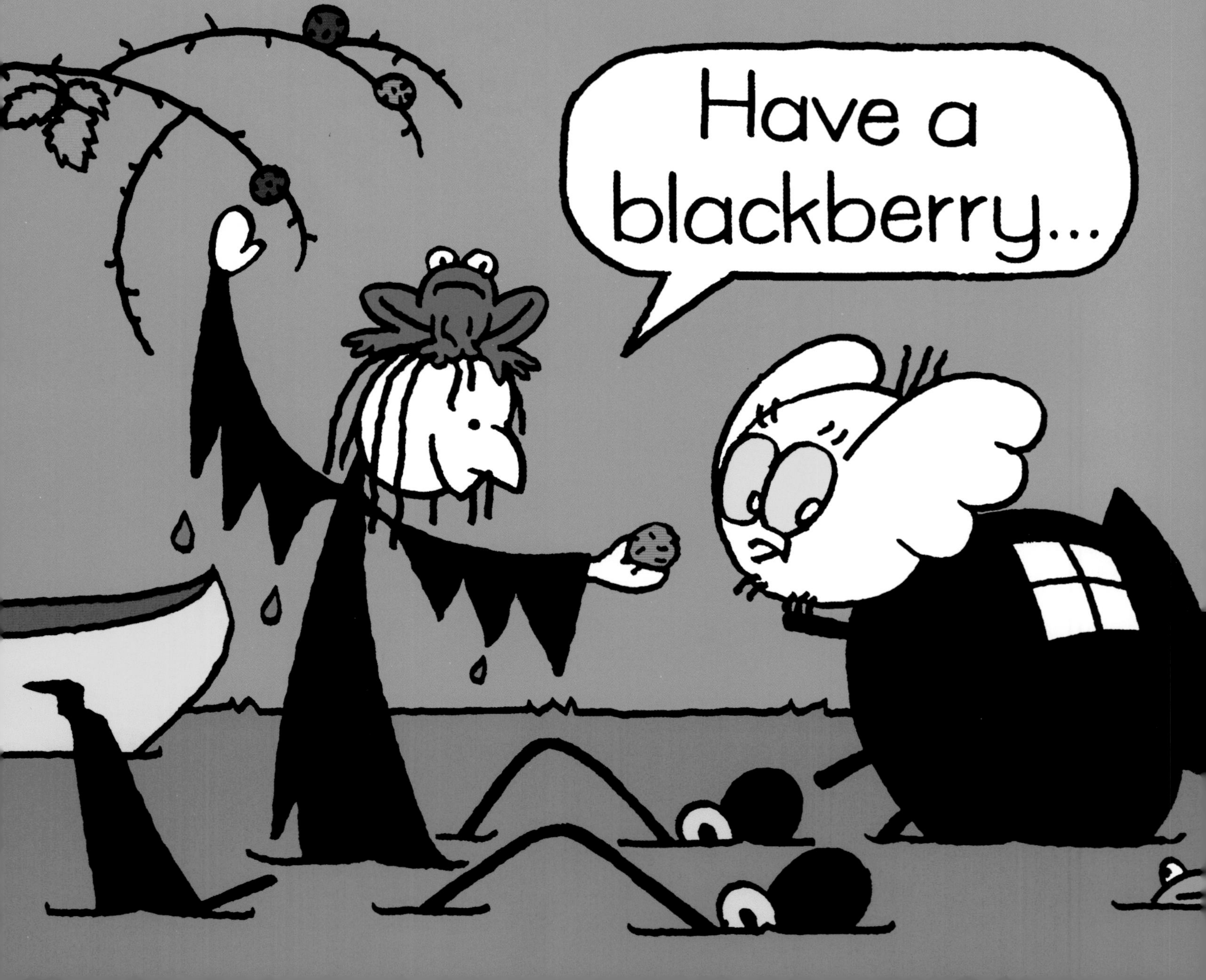
Have a blackberry...

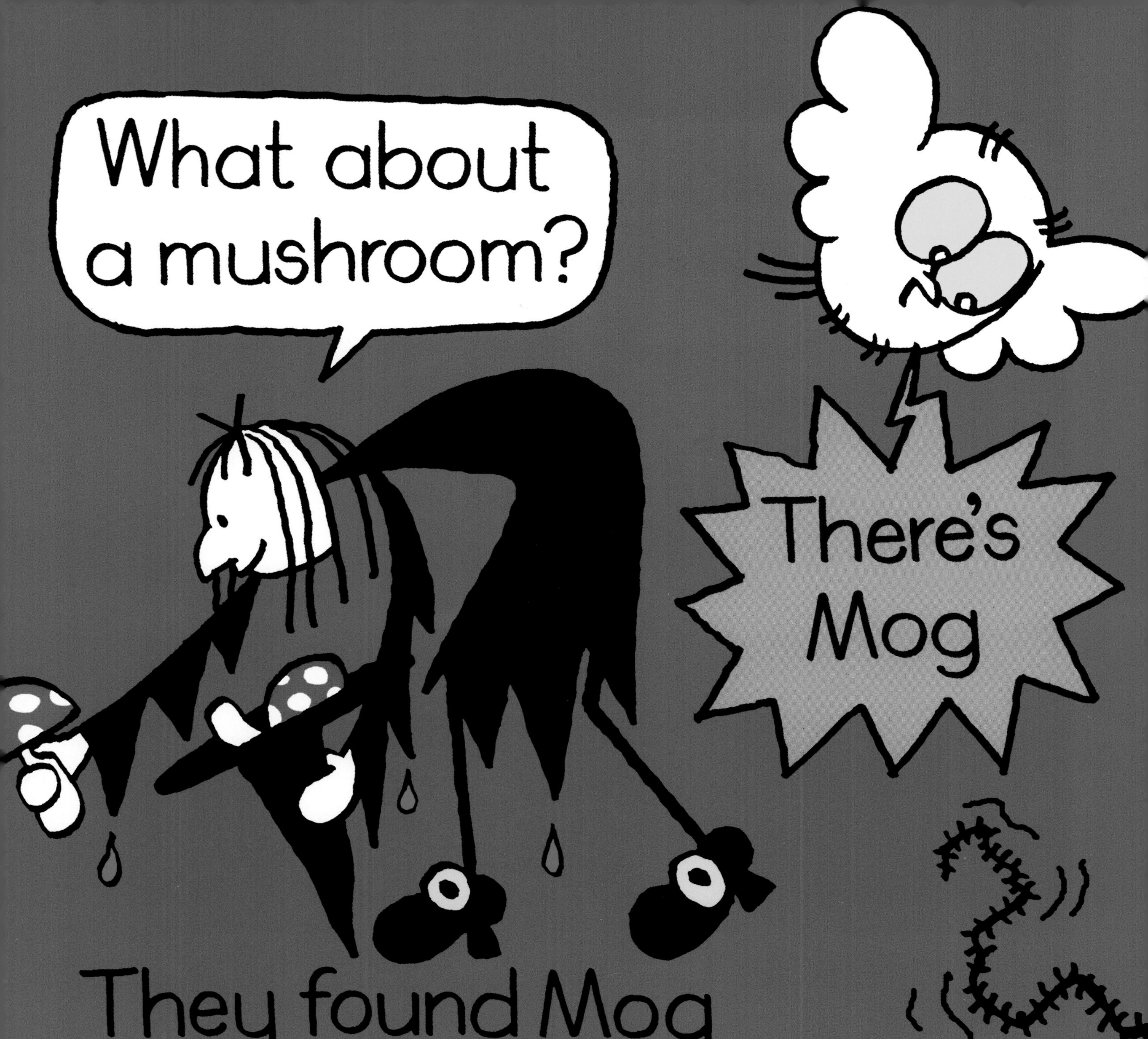
What about a mushroom?
There's Mog

They found Mog

Did you catch anything?
Nearly

I'm starving
Lucky I've got something in the cauldron

They rushed back

What is it?
It's a surprise
Smells funny

It's moving
It's alive
EEEK!
It's a...

FOX!

There goes dinner
We'll starve
Oh dear oh dear

It got dark

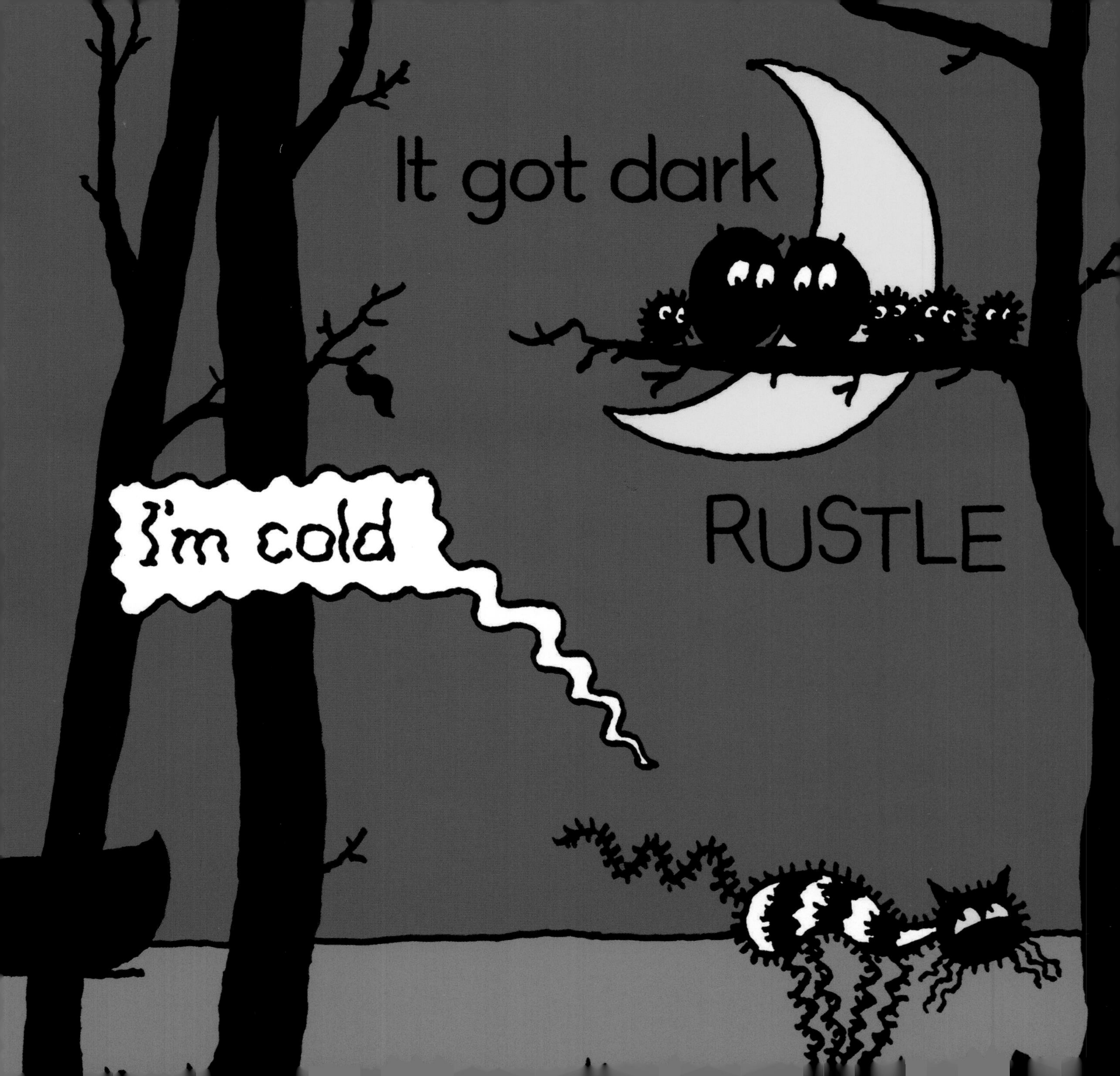
I'm cold
RUSTLE

They heard strange noises

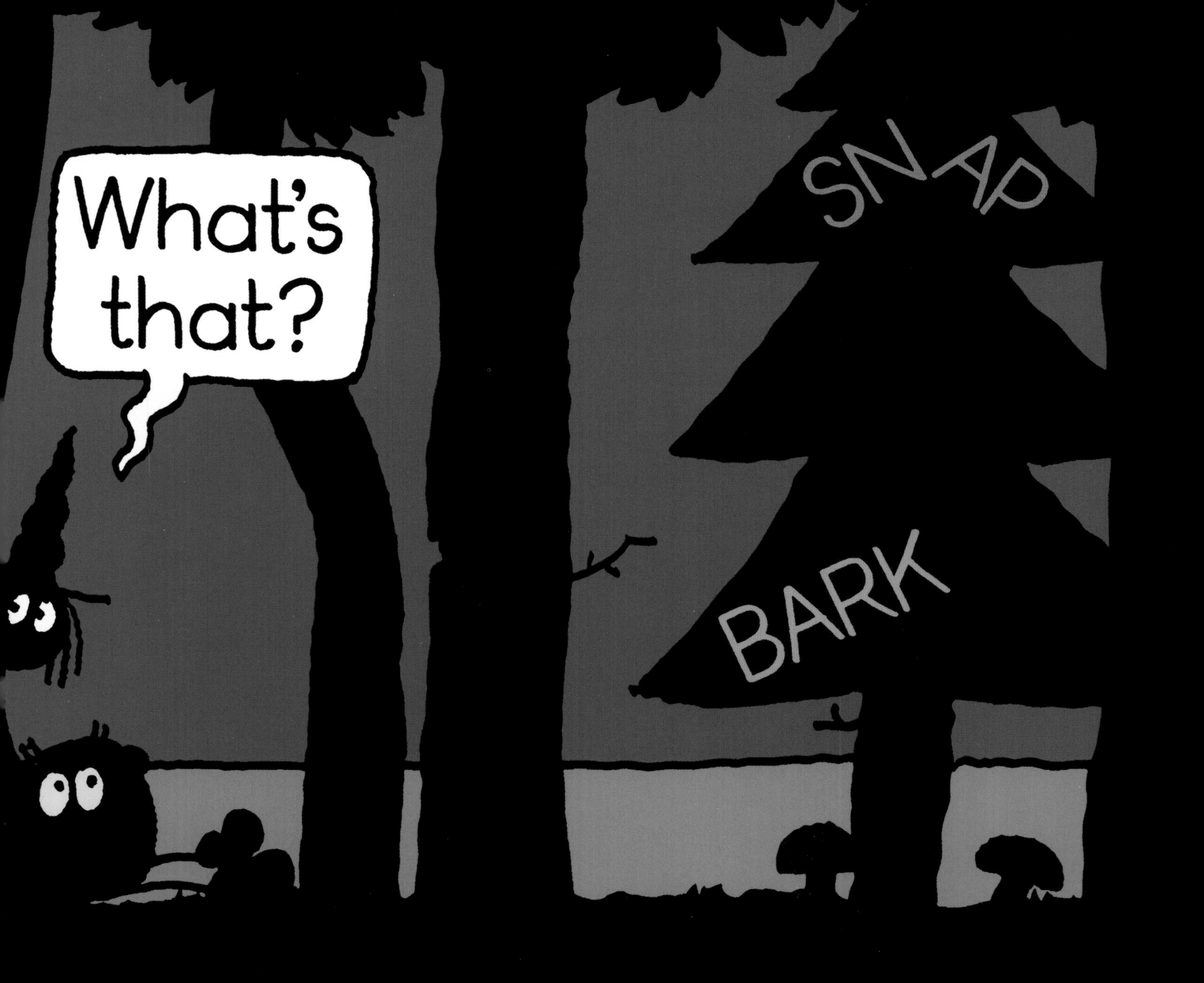
What's that?
SNAP
BARK

The canoe drifted away
How will we get home?

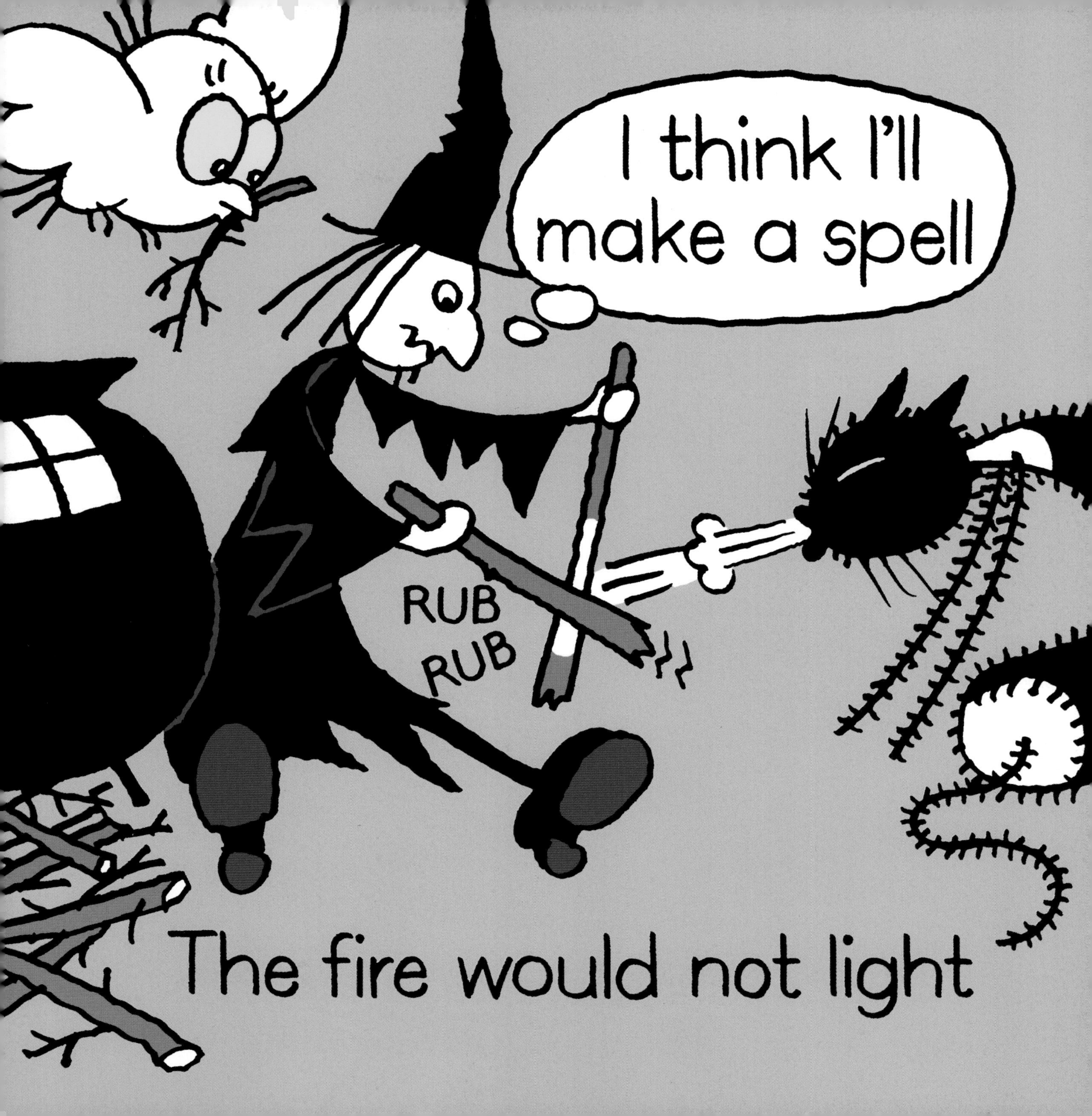
I think I'll make a spell
RUB RUB

The fire would not light

Meg put in
7 snails
4 fire flies
a bird's nest
and a snap dragon

Fire! Fire!
Strike a light
Flash bang wallop
Get a fright

and she made her spell

It went like a rocket

BOOM!!

You called?
Have you got a match?

The fire lit

They all had supper

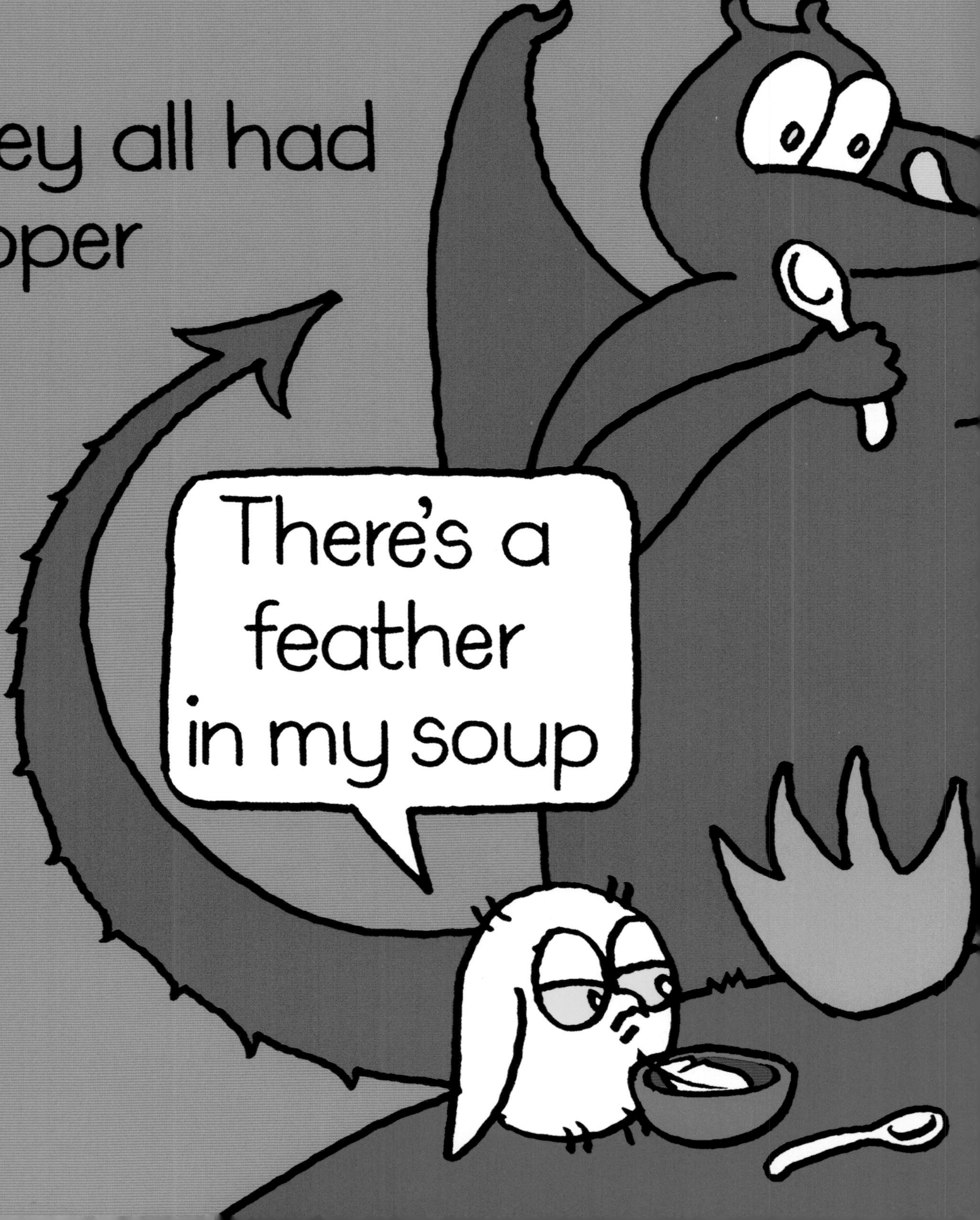
There's a feather in my soup

Can I have some more?
You must come to stay

I hope he doesn't stay too long

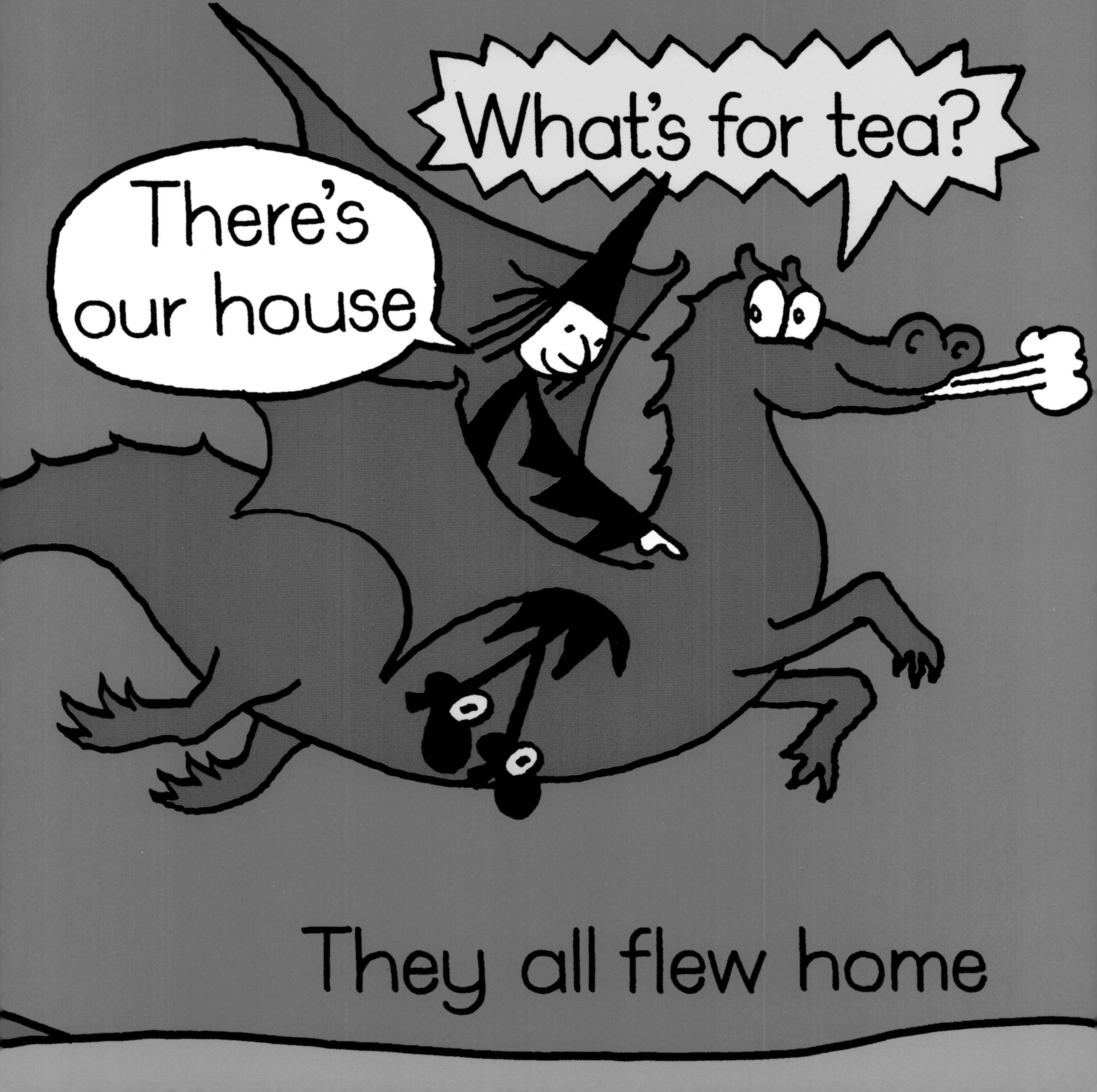
There's our house
What's for tea?

They all flew home

Goodbye!